MW01195562

A CLEAN, WELL-LIGHTED PLACE

August 2011

FOUNDED IN 2011

VOLUME I * NUMBER I

CONTENTS

SUMMER POETRY CONTEST

Executive Editor	ANTHONY BLAKE
Editor	CAROLINE SCHOEFFLER
Editor	DUSTIN BISHOP

COVER ART BY CAROLINE SCHOEFFLER

A publication of *A Clean, Well-Lighted Place*
www.lightedplace.com

Copyright © 2011 by A Clean, Well-Lighted Place
ISBN: 978-1-257-86466-9

POETRY

MARY STONE

After Getting the Mole Removed

We ate hard peaches, wishing we had
picked up the other ones.

These were more like pears, you said,
hard, missing that peach juice.

We ignored the bandage on your left hand,
the shadow of dried blood

that shone through. I imagined the black
mole, scraped off a scalpel

into a clear jar. After, you had to stock up
on sun-block and left-handed gloves.

The doctor would be going over each mole
one by one in the exam room,

every few months; I vowed
to get to them before anyone else –

to linger over them with my breath,
to brush them with the care I would a nipple.

I didn't tell you how it had looked like
the stigma of a flower, how I couldn't

help but wonder if each mole on your pale skin
was made up of a cluster of smaller moles,

if these buds could fall, scatter along

your limbs and make others grow.

I didn't know what pollinated them,
the sun, or the touch of my hand.

Bare Ache

He woke her to say that everything was blue,

the hornet's skin, the bird bath water glowing
in the backyard at night, the creases of her eyelids

bared beneath lamp light. Then he woke her
to describe the growl of motorcycles before sunrise:

they seemed as angry as aged bodies. She said
the riders must have been constant travelers, aching

for warm stones pressed on their backs, the comfort
of cotton and down. She fell asleep imagining

wrinkled hands pulling breaks at stop lights,
boots and asphalt, faces scraped with wind.

He was awake beside her, calm like the dark,
his fingers clawing the sheets.

STEPHEN MEAD

That Harp

Scotland sent in a maiden voyage
of shawls, the embroidered ferns,
the ivy tracery pure as frost
with the lime light silver...
What a sea story in the strings,
the verdant waves of flaxen mead,
and one could hear a sky
encompassing all such loveliness
in a magic carpet ride
of closed lids...

Listen, you who have been history-kicked,
riddled with the doubts of any mid-life,
I give you this harp as tightrope talisman,
as lodestar trapeze.
Unwrap yourself like velvet,
reddest over the gold flake.
Your journey has more notes
to be sure of, your fingers, a footing.
Pluck, play what is good water
added to a fountain.
Strum with what ails you.
My Wild Irish Rose is still a song
for the singing.

TERRI BROWN-DAVIDSON

De Kooning's Women

What I love about monsters is how ghosts float beneath
their shimmering green facades,
the women's teeth bared
though each canine, bicuspid,
isn't a Boschian nightmare
but paint crumbling or high-knifed
on a canvas rife with attacks, with feints at a bastard perfection,
the paint applied thick as defensiveness
then scooped away
until only some skeleton idea remains--
like fog on a San Francisco morning
when you angle three fingers before your face
and hand, eyes, self become
a disappearing act you almost can't bear
because it's beautiful, this obliteration,
as all inevitabilities are, though
whether the destruction is monstrous or real
is difficult to say.

Woman in a wheelchair. Ninety-eight years old.
Not my mother or grandmother, though--hell--they're aging, too,
all of us engaged in this slough,
the cranium, the brain, reduced to a malfunctioning organ,
prone to thought erosion, to stuttering attacks of strangeness
that seem so remote to the soul--
who can even fathom it? A woman in a wheelchair
in a rest home. A woman I was forced to visit, compelled
because I didn't know her--a friend of a friend of an enemy
I can't remember--
and, forty-five years old, I know
mortality makes me squeamish.

She was sitting by a plate-glass display of finches,
a translucency washed white by fluttering sheets of sun,
the birds purple, red, green, a provocative shade of mauve,
emitting throaty chirps as they fluttered from branch to branch.
Her hands glimmered withered and dry, like bone sculptures left out
to brighten on the Mojave floor;
her hands clung to the blistering wheelchair pads.
And her eyes flickered grayish, near-frosted,
opaque, cataracts floating there, a thick tissue
blossoming that pulled her away from the world,
made her a recluse, an object, a blot,
and I wanted to believe, gazing upon her masklike unsentient face,
that it was possible for some separations to be beautiful,
even the final one.

And I know that woman died. Heard she died
months later. She was a thing that outlived its time,
an oversoul that could no longer bloom in a body that'd
shrunk to bone and confine. And,
wandering Manhattan streets at one a.m., two,
a forty-five-year-old woman in a beat-up overcoat,
unprepossessing as any other night creature
who frequents this territory, taking the route
that De Kooning pursued all those nights after bingeing
when he grew hungry then ravenous for something he couldn't name,
Elaine sleeping at home in their big featherbed or screwing
another stranger for the competitive hell of it,
De Kooning longing for something he couldn't evoke
beyond canvas and Blue Ochre and brush, so overflowing
with this <u>something</u> that he couldn't walk straight,
couldn't keep his legs from trembling, and the pinched
arteries and veins and wasting muscles that comprised them--
God, I want it too, whatever ghost of immortality
floats ephemeral inside me

though I can barely detect its presence,
the essence I keep seeking in a world of lacquer, shatter,
the undersoul that can never die.

Arbus as Pieta

I confess it: I'm besotted.
Bring on more grainy, gray-haired men
with flesh trembling slack, with dangling baglike jowels,
with marbled eyes sunk in sockets
that peel away like tissue from veined and sodden cheeks.
Let me snap another bum
lounging in his piss, pretend he's human for a while,
sink to my ripped-jean knees, camera striking
each hardening nipple, prop his head upon my lap
until my shirt fabric reeks.
Let me tell him that he's drinking. Tell him that he's dying.
Let me tell him he's a freak.
Let me tell him that he's me
and I adore him in his rot.

The Mentally Retarded Series: Diana Arbus Captures
Two Glass-Eyed Girls at Play

She stripped off her jeans during each shoot,
needing to feel dark wet soil creep up against her knees,
to savor the muck, the soupy mess, of the soil they'd rolled across
splashing their hands in muddy sinkholes, less sentient than puppies.
Whirling in shredded gingham dresses,
bobby socks crumpling around fat unshaven calves,
their faces browned with muck, they seemed effervescent
as they cartwheeled across frozen-bugged
blunted grass. And how to describe what came next when--
the damp making Diane shiver, whisper, tremble,
the dead-stubble scent that was autumn
in all its red-gold smear and evocativeness
obscuring her ground-grass lens--Diane, glancing up, spotted
one girl, nubbed teeth thrusting up blunt-pale from her gums,
twine her fatted palms
like Bernadette of Lourdes communing with a holy one
while Diane, wiping her lens dryer with one thumb,
waited for her third and clearer eye to flutter open.

JOHN SWAIN

Chained Rock

Mountain stone
kept the sky separate
as clear waters fell
like a woman's hair
onto bare shoulders.
I have neither reason
nor belief
like a chain nailed
into the outcropping
far above the town.

ELOISE SCHULTZ

Danielle at thirty-one

Danielle at thirty-one appears like a lion,
beaming and bearing mettle.
She carries it across her shoulders;
nervously, genially, and
bright beyond belief.

She smiles. Danielle has seen
the continuous algebra of broken parts,
now sealed by the hand of some ineffable.
Dimensions ripple like
a reshuffling cube;
fanning out into something
honest, quiet, persistent.

That a language ever could spell out
coordinates in her cloud atlas, that it could
strip the moon to shy, naked love,
that it could ever dream in the first place.

Danielle smiles. she has seen
something bright again, something
with the potential energy of great resonance.
That a language nesting inside another
with perfect, mathematical symmetry
could plot itself so beatifically in space.

MARK SIMPSON

Jesus Christ in a Green Canoe

The Stillaguamish is flooding
and the Snohomish not far behind.
We go down to watch
from the Fourth Street bridge.

My daughter counts the hay bales.
Someone else is counting cows,
who are swimming furiously for shore,
but the current is just too strong.

Everything upstream has come loose.
Just before the cops shoo us
off the bridge, there he is,
Jesus Christ in a green canoe.

One of the cops yells
but I don't think he hears.
He is pretty good with that canoe.
He keeps it straight despite

the roiling water.
He uses his paddle to
push the floating cows aside.

Roofer on the Way Down

Wholly in air.
On the way down,
a glimpse of gray cedar siding,
a startled robin in a dwarf birch.
Someone walking a dog, carrying a red
paper coffee cup.
He had time to think.
It was as if all
the fumes of the age had cleared,
all the fumes of his life.
It was all hard fact now.
There was no disputing it, no
interpretation other than what it was,
no reification/amplification.
Then the last thing he heard
was his boss, "Larry! Larry! Where
the fuck are you?"

CLARE L. MARTIN

Meditation on "Imitations of Winter II"

After the photograph, "Intimations of Winter II" by Zeralda La Grange

There is a harmony
            in the commingling
of light

            and dark– ghost patterns
formed on
            snow-sodden

ground.   All in stasis, here,
            broken glints

hang mid-air
            and still
                        the cypress rots.

How do we speak
            the dead-etchings
                        of grass?

This artifice,
            in the infinitesimal,

has lost from view
                        the on/off pulse

            of blue-black wings.

The only hint
            of their affect

was held in the breath
                of the artist

and not entrapped
in the gloss

     of this picture.

How It Comes

Sometimes it comes in a sleep
 in which you dream of the blackest horses,

It comes riding on the strong back of the animal,
or is tangled in its mane. Often, it is

itself the glowing coal of an eye,
which burns through you.

Sometimes it comes from the air,
rising from the strangeness of a threatening sky.

Wind exhales it into your ear,
or it seeps through the ground

like the fresh spring;
then it chills us--

It comes in the body of nature, or not.
It is not always a mystery.

It may come to you in the memory
of a city; perhaps San Francisco

or New Orleans or Tucson.
Or in the recollection

of the first and last kiss
of someone you loved, or did not.

Today it came to me
as a bird; its wingbeat

light as a whisper, pecking
fruit in a verdant heart.

MANGESH NAIK

Tree

Shirtless souls : indestructible, zipped up bodies
queue along the fake horizon. One branch and we
are a tree. A wave of tiny wings hits the center
of each leaf. Unappeasable, no matter how many

rain years it takes to rhyme with the soil
Woven between trees, their genealogies
grow protecting us from themselves.
Sunlight articulated into gauzy green cheeks.

Only a few modest strokes of this and that
is how a forest loos like. Rearranging things
under the zooming screens of light. Desecration
of the body over, it's slapdash re-construction

curiously accurate. Rebirth magistrates assemble downhill.
Intensity transcribes into the hill's shadow. Something
changes. The repetition or it's reflection. Ersatz sun
rising and setting randomly in different parts of the sky

In a single, blinding flash. Awestruck, as if awakened
by consequence of imagination. My dawn starts in my
heart of wood. I breathe like someone leaving and then
coming back from the simple black of night

Vanaprastha Party

The question never
left the umbrella

of her feet. I can
tell by the way

she stands. Stunning
bolts of legs

closed. Breathing
air full of coffee.

I sit damp, as if
sewn to myself

Ambushed by the
bottom in the crumpling

of skirts, wordless
woman weapon.

I pinch the air
I wobble suggestive.

Solid translation
of my intent but

the wrinkled mustache
returns broken

point of entry
no longer opens.

DENIS JOE

Liverpool Soap Opera 19
        (after Walt Whitman)

you city of ships
black hulled   sailing on forwards
defying poet *blaggards*
who would applaud your demise

you city of ships
captained by partygoers
dropped off by lifeboat rowers
to seek strangers to baptise

you city of ships
whose crew chant and celebrate
with shanties that explicate
a past you try to revise

you city of ships
sailing a sea of promise
coming out from a darkness
finding a new paradise

you city of ships
it is time to weigh anchor
I will greet you tomorrow
in the glory of sunrise

Liverpool Soap Opera 39

go   get a message
from cecil's   son   as before
mind you don't slip on the floor
tell him I'll settle tuesday

go   get a message
from malones   large bag of chips
salt and vinegared   two fish
come straight home now   don't delay

go   get a message
to your father   son   quick   run
or else his dinner will burn
and mind the road on your way

go   get a message
to sammy   bernard   tell him
there's no money coming in
I'll straighten up next payday

go   get a message
to the priest   ask him to come
I feel life drain from me son
I won't last another day

Liverpool Soap Opera 46

so long renshaw street
how time has ploughed your features
old posters flap like sutures
your pavement is full of waste

so long renshaw street
your yawning greets the new day
and you cannot hide the grey
roots that shoot up from your face

so long renshaw street
your spectacles are defunct
now your selling tat and junk
at a much inflated price

so long renshaw street
so lewis's has closed down
rapid has moved nearer town
and emptiness fills the space

so long renshaw street
the whores from the aldelphi
finding your kerbs too lowly
have left for a better place

penelope waits
the cathedral piazza
holds a reflection of her
slight   distorted by the rain

penelope waits
as if a worn-out clich□
helping to explain away
something that no-one else can

penelope waits
the oath of tyndareus
the source of all this madness
took away   from her   her man

penelope waits
hopeful of the probable
sometimes   inexplicable:
the war in afghanistan

penelope waits
beneath the clock in queen's square
checking her purse for the fare
to take her back home again

JOEL ALLEGRETTI

Yoko Ono[1]

[1] The text is in your mind. Your mind's eye says, "Thank you."

CHRISTOPHER BEARD

Love Abstract with Flood and Secrets

There Are

There are thirty three holes in the sky
flying west, thirty three blackbirds
I see through to the source of rain,
and she wants birds to just be birds,
the sky to remain intact,
a pocket sealed with sun.

There are twenty five jars
where she keeps my hair,
where the curls wrap around
the bending light forever.

There are numberless hours spent damaging
the asphalt, our whole lives lived in a car,
enduring summer's drag, drinking
like it is medicine to cure our heavy blood.

There Were

There were three years of storms back home
waited out in the basement with a bucket and oar,
water filling the window wells as we pretended to sleep
through the swell, burst, and flood,
the disaster growing beneath us
as we floated up through the swampy mud.

There were a few secret things I could not speak of making love
to,
their magic not known to the sky,
to permanence, or motion,
magic unknown to you, your pillow-dress dolls,

your perfumed sheets, the damp sweat
of your sweet soaps.

But what was our perpetual romance
without its fraction of torture?
There were a fistful of reasons
we incessantly slept
in bed as if straightjacketed,
as if my hands were taped to my sides
while all the separate places we had been
 began to converge.

HOWIE GOOD

Hell in a Very Small Place

Houses collapse into the street, clubbed by police. My face looks back at
me for an explanation. Six million point to the numbers tattooed on their
arms. Inside, I'm orange red, raw umber, maize. No plan ever quite works
as designed. One in the morning, dark
and rainy, roses from the South open to reveal a gold front tooth.

Sun in My Window, Rain at My Door

1

A man jammed fistfuls of earth into his mouth. And why not when
nations sell weapons to their enemies? The weather arrived late, a funeral
with only four mourners. All his life he liked to wander through
cemeteries. If everyone is doing it, someone said, it must be OK.

2

Probably the first paint was animal blood. He asked for a razor. The
woods on the outskirts of Jersey City suffered from fever and night
sweats. Everything yearned toward everything else. He was found, six
days later, wearing only one shoe. Some of his sketches from that period
are spattered with raindrops.

3

Born on a cold day, he took with him a heart always about to break. He
picked cherries from the tree and threw them down to her. Eight green
hills overlooked the river. She was there no more than three or four
minutes, her white dress dashed with blood as bright as the cherries she
caught.

JEREMY D. CAMPBELL

Lunch in the Park

I am a curiosity for the bees.
Distant at first, now they come low
across the green blades thin and thick,
wondering at my meaty fragrance.

This blanket is rough, full of faded colors without a pattern.
Not the kind I would have chosen, but the kind left behind.
Do bees see color? Do they ask why
I would care if they do?

A black ant is navigating the nearby grass.
I look away for a moment and lose it,
and recoil when I discover that
the adventurer, barely a thousandth my size, is nearly upon me.

To the crawlers I am a new landscape, sometimes opening
its mouth and blowing them carelessly into the air.
To the bees I am a not-flower, a tall and knotted distraction.
Little fliers become tangled in the hair of my arms.

This is a day for horrors.

Squirrel in the Courtyard

Today I read that chopsticks are maternal.
I probably won't read that tomorrow.

Today I paid $3.95 for 8 ounces and some frothed milk art.
How can I blame the squirrel for not taking me seriously?

Soon I have to call my mother and convince her.
Should I argue that her marriage is not as awful as it is?

This type of day is fine: the clouds erase my shadow.
But it might rain. You know how things cling when it rains.

The squirrel bounces about the courtyard, playing, scrambling,
relentlessly curious.
It peers through windows and doors and forgets them so it may do so
again.

I don't know that I'll be in a greenhouse later, or that I'll fall in love again
tonight.
Her face is not a fixed thing: sometimes her eyes are crookedly placed.

I remember all the wrong things. I forget all the best things.
Cultivate a better amnesia, so that her every arrival is unblunted and
shimmering.

MICHAEL MILBURN

For Example

The sight of him swinging
his braced legs down hallways
or perched on a desk,
orthopedic shoes dangling,
made for the sort of
movie-of-the-week moral
of courage and overcoming
that wasn't lost on teachers, students,
parents, parents of prospective students,
visiting board members.
And if a boy mimicked
or mocked him
and he heard about it,
which he inevitably did,
he turned even that
into a lesson. You could say

he was a born teacher,
born not just with a penchant
for preachiness,
but with a body
outfitted as a kind
of textbook on tolerance.
So it was inevitable
he'd be promoted to Dean
and on the day before Christmas vacation
address the school
with his thoughts
on the holiday,
taking as his text
the story of Rudolph

the red-nosed reindeer,
a troubling parable
about, it seems,
special treatment.
Better that Rudolph
had been allowed
to remain among the herd
than promoted to leader
for his blinking nose.

From the Dean's perspective,
this made sense: how tiring
always to be noticed,
even in a positive way.
The students looked chastened;
this was the kind of thing
they expected from school– everything,
even a goofy Christmas story,
mined for its message. In the faculty room later,
a few teachers rolled their eyes--
"I always liked old Rudolph," one muttered,
while another asked, "He got to pull the sleigh, didn't he?
I thought it was a success story."
I wondered who was at fault,
our colleague for exceeding
his role as example, or us
for revealing the limits of our tolerance,
and whether
even in accepting difference,
we set it apart.

SUMMER POETRY CONTEST

JOHN SWAIN   First Place

Synchrony Lens

Nightfall uncalm and hiding,
I took comfort in splinters
and the bricks of a chimney,
the summer bed grew into moons
below the honeysuckle.

Pinned like red silhouettes
you were invisible as me,
fireflies lanterned the road
beside the traveling stream.

I jumped from a high rock
and the water let me become you,
then I saw your daughter
singing in a different valley
with a seek of whippoorwills.

The proper exercise of sadness

He and his wife had run the restaurant
on the Oregon mountain for thirty years, where
Mexican food never appeared on the menu.

When Maricela died, he did not despair.
There was the restaurant to run, kids in college,
savings to invest. But there was a problem, too:

she had always asked to return to Michoacan,
when things settled down and money permitted.

Now, as he waited for the eggs to fry, facing away
from the hungry gabachos at the counter, and
Augustin sang some old song at the grill,
he allowed himself to rest his head in his hands
and hum along, imagine her hand on his hairy arm,
in the hills where the air rises cool from the ocean.

Big Bang

In the beginning- our television tells us
there was an empty expanse, a vast,
primordial unimaginableness. And a dot.
An energy-dense spot, blotched
upon the open universe. Remote
outstretched, eyes intent, my girlfriend
lowers the volume, while onscreen,
an explosion. Super-novaed from nothing.
Violent shattering, ultraviolet sharding. Random,
says the voice-over. Look, says my girl.
Particles percolate, cartoon protons,
neutrons, electrons. Life- kernels. We chew
popcorn; we watch their birth. Everything
comes down to charges, I say, and my lips
find the hot hollow of her clavicle. Bursts,
meteorites, as matter expands the asteroid
belt, as she unbuckles mine. A wonder,
what eons wrought, what Hadean brought.
From cosmic microwave radiation, Jolly Time
popcorn. From galaxy dust, soap
operas, colors, spam in a can, ethics, aesthetics,
war, love, god. And her touch- the legacy
of some collapsed and unaware star.

FICTION

GEORGE MASTERS

Before You Were Born

San Francisco, California

In the Presidio at night, in a one man tent, Tom Harp dreamed a story. Told and re-told by his mother and father, he heard them tell it together and separately. Over the years, the story grew from a boy's coloring book to a Jack London short story, to a Hemingway novella. And always, even from the beginning, he saw it as a movie, a film rich with detail, voice and music.

Mother and Father telling it at the dinner table, Father grilling steaks in the snow and driving him to hockey practice, Mother on a beach, Father in a bar, and so it went. In a row boat, at the sink washing dishes, over a chess game, on the veranda of a grand hotel in Zurich, splitting wood in Maine and fishing off the rocks. He heard the story once on the last train out of Hoboken, eating hot dogs with the old man, the two of them alone in the smoking car with mustard on their knuckles. Sober, sometimes maybe not so sober, the story always began, "Before you were born...."

In the tent, Harp groaned in his sleep. Knees to his chest, wrapped in a poncho liner, the night wrapped tight around his shoulders. Before the dream began, he felt that jolt, the sudden drop and stop, when a sleeping man catches himself just before falling. Through a train window the size of a movie screen, Harp watched the dream unfold. Leaning into it and looking up, finding everyone alive and larger than life, he swam to the dream and became part of it.

The Caribbean Sea, December 1945

Aboard the Marguerite, the forty four foot ketch Grandfather built, they are somewhere west south-west of St. Vincent. In his mother's belly, Harp can smell the sea. He can feel and hear it. Outside, there is fresh daylight. The easy rise and fall of the boat is to ride the watery keep. The wind and current spark his heart. His mother's humming tickles an ear lobe. She shifts a hip to get more comfortable and it makes him kick.

Pregnant on deck, Eleanor Harp drinks a cold beer. The tanned and handsome Navy doctor in Key West told her beer was better for the boy than coffee.

"A boy?"

"Yes, I believe so." The doctor had close cut grey hair, half a left thumb and an eye patch. The good eye was grey with specks of brown and green.

She said, "Really?"

"Unofficially, yes."

He told her the joke about the Italian doctor and the nun while he finished his examination. Eleanor laughed. Emboldened, she asked about the eye.

He shrugged it off. "Battle of Midway. My son thinks it makes me look like a pirate."

Trying to imagine his son, her heart took a spin. She almost said something but caught herself and changed direction. She wanted to know more about beer being healthy for the unborn lad. The doctor explained that in moderation, consider it liquid food.

"Can I start knitting in blue?"

The patch and the good eye admired her navy, pin striped skirt. "That's a safe bet. But just in case, blue also looks good on young ladies."

On the forward deck of the Marguerite, Eleanor pictures the doctor and how the half thumb came down the side of his jaw when he smiled. Remembering the Christmas party in Key West, she hums, "Silent Night". She knows it's a German song but loves it anyway. Breathing the bright late morning and northeast trades, she feels the primal kick of her unborn sailor. Up near the bow, legs dangling over the side, arms behind her, palms flat on the hard smooth teak, she angles her face to the sun.

Grandfather Smith, tall and broad shouldered, stands at the helm. Patrick Harp, five years old, stands next to his grandfather. A hand on a spoke of the wheel, Patrick pretends he's steering. Draining the last swallow from a bottle of Coca-Cola, Patrick burps.

From time to time, Grandfather sweeps the sea with the big black Navy binoculars that hang from his neck. At the stern, his father, Lt.

Commander Gordon Harp, sits on a fish box. Feet up on the transom and lost in thought, he fishes.

The war is over. The Caribbean Sea is clear of German U-Boats but not the mines. Black, stiff fingered balls, the patient machines float lazy and wait. On calm days, the rogue mines take to rolling and sunning themselves on the surface. After a storm, they have a tendency to wash about and come ashore. When they don't explode a fishing boat or blow a hole in a reef, they lay up on the beach like ugly tourists from another planet.

Grandfather is mahogany brown. Thick necked and heavy around the middle, he wears shorts and a torn white T-shirt. Pulling the long billed fishing cap low over his eyes, he wipes the sweat beading at the base of his great bald skull.

Grandfather measures the wind and gauges its mood. The Atlantic zephyr that last touched land in the Canary Islands is now arriving in the West Indies. Being late December, the northeast trades come up out of the southeast at 17 knots. After its long trip across the ocean, the wind seems pleased to be among islands. Perhaps a little tired today but why not? Taking time to breathe, to gust and stream, the wind is relaxed enough to enjoy the sun and warm water, acting that way as it fills the sails and ruffles the surface.

Making eight knots, the Marguerite is angling down across the north equatorial current. Looking up from the compass, Grandfather raises his head to the horizon. The senior vice president of a Pennsylvania steel company has the leathered face of an old catcher's mitt. As a young man working in the plant, he burned off his fingerprints rolling steel. His company made the heavy armor for battleships and cruisers. Still, the Germans and Japanese sank his ships. Shovel-jawed, legs like trees, a potato nose and no fingerprints, he lowers his eyes to scan the troughs and crests for mines.

Fishing off the stern, Gordon Harp wears naval aviator sun glasses, a pair of faded khakis, no shirt and tennis shoes. Firing up a Lucky Strike, he pulls back on the fishing rod. The smoke soothes him. The fishing line strums like a guitar string. In a practical manner, he notices the fillets of light that skip across the blue, white veined sea. He enjoys the carnival parade of trade wind cumulus on the horizon. In the cloud formations he sees elephants and dragons, covered wagons and a fat lady dancing. An alligator turns into a string of camels that becomes a giant frog that divides into haystacks. Their bottoms cut flat, the cotton haystacks pile up as towering chimneys.

Gordon Harp smokes and bares his teeth. If one didn't know him, the expression might pass as a grin. Out of habit, he radars the sky and cuts it into quadrants. He's looking for that first grain of pepper, a dark spot coming out of the sun that in two blinks can become a Mitsubishi torpedo bomber. He's also on watch for the giveaway flash of sun on a Zero's windscreen. No Japanese in this sky and he knows it. Thinking about spotting one anyway, he finds himself returned to the Pacific.

Guadalcanal, Saipan, Tinian and Iwo Jima. Tarawa with the damn changing tides. Marines in landing craft caught on the coral reefs at low tide, stuck there and taking awful losses. Marines and sailors getting chewed up in a cross fire from Japanese gun emplacements hidden in caves above the beach.

Forgetting the cigarette, he sees amphibious tractors and landing craft disappear in red geysers. He smells Marines floating in the lagoon and washing up on the beach. Bloated, ravaged by sun and fish and crabs, they had to lay there for two days because enemy gun fire made it impossible to retrieve them.

Gordon Harp unable to walk a beach in Honolulu, or Key West without seeing dead Marines half buried in sand, their eye sockets eaten and empty, helmets strewn along the water's edge. Solitary behind the sunglasses, the cigarette has burned down to his chapped lips. Flicking it into the sea, he tongues the burn and lights another. Fishing off the stern, the sun hot on his knuckles and chest, he lets the gurgling wake take the memories. Thinking maybe he can catch a tuna or a snub nose dolphin, he gazes at the patterns of dried fish blood on lace-less tennis shoes.

Below deck, the radio picks up whistling static. Radio transmissions, hyphenated by squeaks and crackles, are inexplicably replaced by the clear reception from a British island radio station. Glen Gray's Casa Loma Orchestra plays, "Pennsylvania Six Five Thousand". On a day like this, alone at sea, the music emerges from the salon as it would in a movie.

On deck, Eleanor especially likes the part where the band joins in and sings the telephone number. Kicking long brown swimmer's legs off the port side makes her think of dancing. She remembers how Gordon looked in dress whites at the Officer's Club. Before the war, his eyes spent a lot of time on her. And now he couldn't sit still, his eyes always jumping from this to that. His gaze moving from her face to an invisible something behind her, from complimenting her earrings, to checking his fingernails, from her hair, to their son on the carpet making engine noises with a toy truck, to a car passing on the street and then to a faraway nothing. The war gave Gordon nightmares and changed his mouth. Yes, he could smile when he had to, but the boyish grin was gone.

Sun penetrates Eleanor's bare shoulders and the sea spray cools her feet. Drinking a Red Stripe, she presses the cool brown bottle to her cheek. She feels her baby turn on his side and flutter kick. Bless his heart, he's trying to swim. Yes, this boy certainly is an adventurer. The boat rises and falls to the ocean's rhyme while his mother cushions the roll.

Grandfather shouts, "Mine!" Shouting it again, he points. Gordon drops the fishing pole and stands to look. He sees it. Hustling wife and son below, he comes scrambling back on deck with the M-1 rifle and an extra clip.

Stepping on to the salon roof, he locates the mine. Keeping his eye on the mine, he loads the rifle and allows the bolt to slam home. Using the rifle's sling as a brace, he leans up against the mainmast, thumbs off the safety and takes aim.

Less than seventy yards off the starboard beam, the deadly, black spiked ball trails a nest of kelp and lolls in the sun. With the Marguerite rising and falling, the mine is briefly exposed then drops into a trough to hide.

Gordon Harp blinks at the sweat in his eyes. His heart is booming and he can't stop the tremor in his arms. Waiting to get the rhythm of his sight picture, he fires and misses. Below deck, Eleanor turns up the radio. The British station is playing a Lone Ranger record. As the William Tell Overture ends, she makes loud horsey sounds and bounces Patrick on her knee.

Gordon Harp wipes at his right eye with the knuckle of his trigger finger. Feeling the rattle in his knees, his second and third shots lay flat and echoless.

Grandfather keeps the boat close to the wind to give his son-in-law a steady platform. Spotting with the binoculars, he shouts, "Your last was about six feet short and three to the left."

Gordon Harp takes a deep breath and releases half of it. It is quiet enough for him to hear the Lone Ranger shooting it out with the bad guys. Strangely, the shaking leaves his arms. Sighting where he thinks the mine will appear, the rise and fall of the boat comes up between his legs. Waiting for the moment, just before the mine will be fully exposed, he sees the tips of the black tentacles appear and squeezes off the shot. The sea explodes a thunderous column of salt water, steel and smoke.

Shrapnel falls into the sea and around the boat. Smelling the explosive charge and smoke, Grandfather squints at the hazed spot where the mine had been. Gordon Harp blinks as smoke drifts across the boat. Pieces of the mine land on deck like steel bird shit. Grandfather, a church-going Episcopalian, shouts things his daughter has never heard him say. Gordon Harp licks chapped lips and unloads the rifle. After several minutes, sea and sky are left without a trace of the Goddamn, fucking kraut mine.

******

In Havana, on the third of March, in a bedroom with a ceiling fan, a balcony and a view of the harbor, Grandfather had a stroke and died in his sleep. On April 21, at three days old, Thomas Harp was taken from the hospital in Portland, Maine to the fishing village of Biddeford Pool. Face to a cold wind, the ocean was grey and rough the first day he laid eyes on it. Bundled in blue knitted boots and cap, wrapped in a blue knitted blanket, his father held him to his chest. Pointing to the waves crashing on rocks, his father's lips brushed his face. "Look at that, Tommy boy, Boom-boom, what do you think of that?"

JOE CLIFFORD

In Cases Such as These

It had been a bad season for hurricanes down south, remnants from late season storms making their way up the coast almost every other week. I was already in a lousy mood– New York City rush-hour traffic on a rain-soaked Monday morning can do that to you– when I got the call from my wife.

"Who's Stanley?" Rebecca asked.

"Just some drunk Denise married on a bender. A long time ago. He's a nobody. A bum."

"You never told me your mother remarried."

"Why would I? It was short-lived, before the whole born again thing. I was a kid. Besides, you never met Denise. It wouldn't have made any sense. And Stan isn't the kind of guy you want to remember."

Traffic crawled, drivers needlessly switching lanes, trying to jockey position.

"Why would he list you as a next-of-kin? The woman at the hospital called you 'his son.' I don't mean to sound crass, Bill, but if he is dying, a lot of times these places look for family to foot the funeral expenses."

The sewers overflowed, torrents carrying empty cigarette packs and hot dog wrappers down the gutter. From their cars, people screamed into the rain, laying on their horns, as if that would make anything better.

"Just promise you'll talk to me before you agree to anything," Rebecca said.

"Before you get worked up, let me call and find out what's going on."

I had my wife give me the number for the nursing home, which was back in my hometown of Baltimore.

Honestly, they could bury him in the backyard for all I cared.

I phoned once I got into the office. The woman I spoke with at Chalice Manor said Stan had recently been admitted, homeless and destitute. Cancer. A very short time to live.

"We had a difficult time tracking you down, Mr. Simms," the woman said.

"I've had the same address for years."

"No, it's not that. You two don't have the same last name."

"Why would we?" I fiddled with some folders on my desk.

"As Mr. Jenkins's only living relative, there are some decisions that have to be made."

"I'm not his relative. I mean, we're not related. He's just some guy my mother met in a bar twenty years ago. He isn't my father. He isn't even my stepfather."

"Is your mother still alive?"

"No, she's not." I saw I had two calls holding. I felt a headache coming on, and I immediately regretted calling these people back. "I haven't had any contact with Stan since they split up. This wasn't even a real marriage."

"They weren't married?"

"No, they were married, but my mother wasn't exactly herself. I don't know what you expect me to do."

"Mr. Simms, we're sorry to inconvenience you. This is a formality. When somebody is as sick as your fath– as Mr. Jenkins– we try to make every attempt to contact all relevant parties. Of course, anything you do is up to you. Given your relationship, you are not financially responsible to do anything. In cases such as these– "

"Cases such as these?"

"Transients. The State allocates a small stipend to handle expenses."

Outside my window on the twenty-seventh floor the skies churned dark, rains turning heavier. The sound of water pelting the glass made my head throb.

"Mr. Simms?"

"How long does he have?"

"The cancer has spread from his liver to his lungs. We think it's probably in the brain, as well. He has been delusional lately. As I said before, without insurance there is only so much we can do."

I told her there wasn't much I could do. I certainly couldn't take the time off work, and, frankly, I had no interest in seeing the man. I said if she needed to have something signed, fax it up, and after I had our lawyers take a look at it, I'd be happy to help.

The morning dragged miserably. I don't know whether it was the storm or the headache or what, but I began remembering things I did not want to remember. I had no desire to revisit those times, dragging my mother out of some neighbor bar, all the birthdays I missed, opening up the refrigerator on Christmas Day to find nothing but some plastic beer rings and mustard.

Around noon I gave up trying to get any work done. The wind and rain lashing against the glass bore into my brain like a dental drill.

I took three aspirin and collected my things.

*

Stan wasn't the first bad decision my mother made; he wouldn't be the last. When he moved into our apartment, Denise was a real head case, and the two of them together were a disaster. Unemployed, stinking drunk, OTB sheets in hand, Stan was forever scouting a shortcut to easy money.

He treated me OK. He didn't hit me or anything. He'd get a little belligerent when he'd had a few too many, but that's not why I hated him. I hated Stan for what he was: a loser. You could smell failure on him the moment he walked into a room. Everything about him screamed desperate, pathetic. Even his face– features all pushed together, cheesy strip of mustache, thinning hair, bulging, thyroid-ravaged eyes, soft chin – betrayed him for what he was: a small-time hustler looking for a free ride.

My mother eventually got straightened out and kicked Stan to the curb, and we resumed our lives. Though her remedy of religion wasn't much better. Like everything else she tackled, Denise had been fanatical about it. Give her credit: when my mother found some new direction, she went at it full tilt. Counseling teen runaways. Native American holistic medicines. To the Lord Jesus Christ himself.

*

Coming into Baltimore, I cut across Highway 40 and up the Jones Fall Expressway. As I neared West 41st Street, I phoned Rebecca.

"Baltimore? You promised you'd call before you did anything!"

"It's a formality. I'm the only person with any connection to the man."

"So now we have to foot the bill?"

"We are not footing anything. They need a signature."

"They couldn't fax something up?"

"A man is dying, he asked to see me, it seemed the least I could do."

"Unbelievable. Yesterday, I'd never even heard of this Stan. Then some woman calls, says he's your father, and then suddenly he's not your father, and then he's this drunk you hate and blame for your mother – "

"I don't blame anybody for my mother." I should've made the call earlier, or not all. The rain fell hard; signs and streets whizzed by. "I can't do this right now. I'm driving through Baltimore in the middle of a goddamn hurricane and I can't see a thing."

There was a long pause.

"Bill, are you having an affair?"

"What?"

"Are you seeing someone else?"

"Jesus Christ! You took the phone call yourself!"

"This just seems weird. This all seems too weird. You're acting strange."

I told her to call the hospital and have me paged if she wanted to run tabs on me. Then I hung up my cell and turned the damn thing off.

The Chalice Manor Nursing Home was rundown and dilapidated. A single story unit with drab brick faÇade, it was clearly State-funded.

Walking up from the tiny parking lot, I imagined the smell of poverty and wretchedness inside, and I immediately wished I hadn't come.

A man and a woman smoked by the automatic front doors under thin plastic awning, rainwater dripping down. The man was in a wheelchair. He didn't have any hands, holding a cigarette butt with trembling, bony stumps. Overweight, his body was shapeless. Like Jell-O outside a mold, he melted into the contour of his chair.

As I passed, the woman muttered something to me. She wasn't in such hot shape herself, onion paper skin and tiny bird frail.

"Excuse me?"

"I ain't seen you here before." When she spoke her left eye twitched.

"I'm here to see someone."

"Oh. It's nice to meet you. I'm Sandy."

She offered me a hand. When I walked inside I almost turned around and apologized. Only I didn't know what I was supposed to be sorry for.

I told the chunky African American woman sitting at the reception desk whom I wished to see. She looked in a book, then pointed down the hall.

The place stank like a morgue, not that I had ever been in a morgue, but I imagined that's the way death would smell: fetid and stale, like a mix of septic solvents, ointment, and warm microwaved food.

I recognized him instantly, despite all the years. He had the same squirrelly face, only smaller, more shriveled.

Stan lay in bed with the covers bunched at the footboard, his head propped on a pillow so he could watch the tiny black and white television bolted to the dresser. He was naked except for a diaper, and his skin was dark yellow and covered with large purple splotches. I couldn't help but feel some sympathy for the man. He may have been a drunk, but, Jesus, to go out like that.

Stan turned his head. It bobbled, too large for his withered body, like a melon impaled on a skinny stick. He stared at me, squinting. A smile formed slowly, exposing a mouth without teeth.

Another man lay a few feet away. He looked retarded, with one of those Down syndrome faces, eternally youthful but dulled. He had his own TV, which was much larger and in color.

"Oh, Billy," Stan said. "I'm so glad you came."

I grabbed a chair and sat down. I tried to summon some of the hatred I'd felt all these years, but it was tough to do so in the face of something so pathetic.

"Can you give me a hand?" Stan asked. He had slid down the bed, his thin legs twisted in the sheets.

I untangled him, reached under his arms and pulled him up. His slack skin hung off the bone like moist meat in a smoker.

Stan retrieved his teeth from a plastic cup on the nightstand. When he snapped them in place, they made a clomping sound, like a horse's hoof.

"How are you, Stan?" It was a stupid thing to say, but I couldn't think of anything else.

"Aw, they got me pretty banged up, kid." He coughed hard, and lifted some tissue to his mouth to sop up the bright yellow phlegm.

I fixed on his protruding stomach and ribs. He looked like one of those starving kids on television, swollen balloon belly, a cartoon.

"Hey, you remember that trip we took to Carlyle's?" he said.

Funny, I'd forgotten about that. This one weekend, he, Denise, and I had driven up to Carlyle's Game Farm, a rinky-dink animal reserve out in the country. They had goats, sheep, cows, that sort of thing. You could feed and pet them.

"Remember when that goat bit your leg?"

Yeah, I remembered. I'd been feeding a goat with those pellets you buy for a quarter from gumball machines, and when I ran out of food, the goat stuck his snout through a hole in the fence and clamped onto my pant leg and wouldn't let go.

"You started crying and your mother grabbed that ranger. You remember? She grabbed him by the collar and screamed right into his face, 'Your goat is eating my boy!'"

I had to smile.

Talking about my mother, a light returned to his eyes, his face less sallow. "God, I loved her. And, oh, how she loved you. It was always,

'Billy can do this' and 'Billy did that.' She was a good woman, your mother. A beautiful woman."

Then Stan's face suddenly turned grave. He looked toward the door, smile gone. "You got to get me outta here."

"And go where?"

"To the money. It's at my place." He checked the door again, then back at me. "Millions," he said in a whisper.

"Millions, eh? Stan, you can't leave."

"You don't understand. We got to get that money!"

"What money?"

"I won the lottery. I got sixteen million stashed in my apartment." He began rubbing his hands. "Oh, we'll be living high on the hog."

"Sixteen million dollars?"

"It used to be two million, but it's five million more each day. They add to it, see? So you got to get me outta here. The girl downstairs is going to steal it. She's got a key." He grimaced, breathing heavier and coughing again.

I told him I'd be right back.

"Eighteen million, Billy!"

"I'm Bill Simms," I said to the nurse sitting behind the desk. "I'm a friend of Stanley Jenkins. Could you give me some information on his condition?"

The woman huffed and spun in her swivel chair. She faced a rack of files on a rolling cart, extracted a large olive green folder and sifted through it. "He's very sick."

"Yes, I know, but– he's talking crazy."

"We're not at liberty to discuss anything except with family members."

"Technically, I am his son, his stepson."

"Oh. The cancer has spread to his brain."

"He said he won the lottery."

The woman laughed. "Sweetheart, if he had any money, he wouldn't be here."

I didn't smile back.

"I'll see if I can find his worker."

I know how money works. I understand it well– I deal with it all day long– but this place smacked of inhumanity. The ward was more like the slum hotels along the Fells Point bowery than a health care facility, floors filthy, dust balls and cobwebs in every corner, black mildew between the cracks. I looked in the other rooms, every one the same: sick, old people on beds, staring at the goddamn ceiling, no one hooked up to anything.

A woman came around the corner.

"Mr. Simms? I'm Mary. We spoke this morning on the telephone. We didn't think you'd be making the trip."

"I changed my mind."

"Why don't you come into my office where we can talk?"

I followed, passing disengaged lighting units on their backs with wires and tubes poking out. Several stuffed black trash bags leaked God-knows-what.

We entered a tiny, cramped office. She directed me to take a seat.

"What were you expecting, Mr. Simms?"

"I don't know. Not this."

"As an administrator here, part of my job is to make final arrangements. Are you familiar with any homes in the area?"

"Homes?"

"Funeral homes."

"The man isn't even dead yet."

"Mr. Jenkins is a very sick man. We can give him some over-the-counter meds, Tylenol, aspirin, but nothing to treat the cancer. His liver hardly functions at all. I can contact the home we normally use."

"And then what?"

"What do you mean?"

"That's it? No...nothing? No service or– ? I mean, Jesus, what is this place?"

"I'm sorry, Mr. Simms, I am a little confused. This morning, you made it clear you didn't wish to have a service."

I pressed my thumb hard against my temple and closed my eyes. Tepid air hissed out of a clanking air conditioner, suffocating the room; you could hear the winds outside.

"Mr. Simms?"

I extracted my checkbook from my inside pocket. I signed my name and tore out the check. "You can fill out the rest."

"I'm sorry?"

"Whatever he needs to be treated like everyone else. So that's he's comfortable, buried like everyone else. Please, just take care of it."

I needed to get some air. Walking toward the exit, I thumbed my cell phone on. It beeped several times and I knew they were all calls I had missed from Rebecca. A cold, hard wind blew the front doors open, and the overhead lights flickered. Sandy and the Jell-O man were not outside smoking. The rain had not let up.

I turned around and headed back to Stan's room.

He had slid down the bed again, all twisted up in the sheets. I straightened him out and propped him back up.

"We going to get the money, Billy?" he asked.

"Not yet," I said, sliding the chair closer and taking his hand. "I want you to tell me about my mother some more."

"Oh," he said, smiling. "God, she was beautiful."

EDDIE JONES

Catlynnite

The moment I set eyes on Catlynn, I readily admit my dainty blush. She told me everything, and it was captivating. Once, she exclaimed in a shudder of horror her views on my belief in the supernatural, which is maybe.

It is ambiguity, she says.

I say, what is.

I am obliged to explain, using parentheses, my position. It is one of opportunity and expenditure. There is a god, I say, and he is well-bearded.

Drenched in shame and sun color, I admit that there are things I don't know about my own soul, also maritime trade.

You are a watchtower, I tell her, long and unsteady.

I can feel the rush of adrenaline, the fear, racing through my veins, the pulmonary and umbilical, both of which carry oxygenated blood, which is decent of them.

Breathing heavily, sweat trickling down the unwashed crack of my oddly pale (noticeably toned) buttock, I slip a hand into the front of her trousers and cradle like a baby her mons pubis.

My finger slides from hair to skin, from black to pink, and I think is this what my mom's feels like. Rising inside of me is a jealousy for my father I thought I'd never feel; outside of me, my penis. Its head is now the size of anyone's foot.

She squirms. The responsibility now falls on me to treat her center with the utmost care and attention and, if necessary, open hostility. Being the man I am, hand nimble as a thief's, I remove myself from her panties, just short of bliss, thank her for a wonderful evening, and retreat from the door in which I came. Slow motion belongs here, but high-pitched, dissatisfied babbling is all I get.

I stop, embarrassed. The pressure of the situation has gotten to me.

Fumbling for words, I tell her: The only long-term consequence of spending money at a clothing store is a sports jacket.

The air is filled with listenable music.

I resort to generosity, to selfless lovemaking. In the end, I feel like glass (brittle) and I feel glass (my hand is on it).

Her screams of ecstasy are loud, not unlike two or three trucks passing by.

We wither, unlike the right kind of flower.

The moment has come for me to go forth and become animated. I speak slowly, in a hush, because there is time for it.

Once, when I was alive on earth, I said, I felt like Monday, as in I felt twenty four hours long, not six feet.

She says, you seem, as of now, very American.

This room has a particular odor. It is one of sweetly fragranced, discarded into an unseen corner, corn-husked shit. My nose is offended, but not unhelped, for I have pinched it.

I have felt the terror of a goat teat, I say. I have become accustomed to its follicle-tipped nozzle of life and leaks of mammary, have closed mine eyes in a bath of its pungent scent.

In this I mean, of course, that I have seen the new pirates movie and it is ridiculous.

My fingers twitch. My hands are completely shot, wrinkled by too much time or bath water, often read by women in turbins. She reaches for them. It dawns on me to not fight it, to leave my hand held.

Perhaps I represent an ingenious youth, I say.

Perhaps you don't, she says.

I select conversational brilliancy or feminine vagary as my after-dinner entertainment. It's so exciting that my mighty shaven jowl drains to the white of wine.

In the morning, the redness of my cheeks will be humbling. Like an ovoid Jonah Hill, I will wake, I will stretch, I will begin my ambulation.

If this were longer, it would be a fifty page tribute to feeling good about decisions.

BRUCE HARRIS

No One in a Public Restroom

No One stands near the first sink, or the far left sink when facing all six sinks. A man spits into urinal nine before urinating. No One understands. No One spits. Automatically flushing two seconds after the man turns, urinal nine is the right-most urinal when facing urinal row. The man approaches the sixth sink and cups his hands underneath the automatic faucet. Water flows. No One watches the man wash his hands, take two steps across the deco-tiled floor, and wave his wet hands in front of one of the automatic paper towel dispensers. Before a paper towel is fully discharged, No One sees the man rip it from its dispenser, leaving about five inches of dangling paper towel. No One likes the bathroom at the city's bus depot. It has old world charm coupled with the latest in electronic plumbing technology. No One survived urological surgery a year prior. No One stares at the door where the man has exited the restroom. Above the door handle is an "L" shaped gadget and an instructional sign explaining to departing restroom patrons the wisdom of using same, opening the door with a forearm, thus avoiding placement of their freshly washed and presumably germ-free hands on the bacteria-ridden door handle. No One notices everyone complies. No One thinks it's the world's cleanest restroom door handle.

No One spends Tuesday observing how men space themselves at the nine urinals, always leaving an empty urinal between themselves and other users whenever possible. The two end urinals, numbers one and nine, receive the most urine and saliva. No One has a stopwatch to measure urination duration. No One notes which urinals are selected. No One detects a rhythm to the sounds of the automatic flushing, water running and paper towel dispensing. No One wonders about the cleanliness of the "L" shaped forearm door gadget, especially because it is summer and most men use their exposed forearm to open the door. No One wonders about bacteria on forearms.

No One moves to a urinal next to one already in use. No One measures the duration of the patrons' urine flow. More data. Interesting data. Different data! No One is replicating a study that was discussed in psychology class years ago. No One thinks about possibilities in elevators and on escalators.

Once the penises are out, No One records the time it takes for urination to begin. No One stands several feet away, unobtrusively. No One observes most men pay little attention to their surroundings, thereby making the restroom the perfect experimental lavatory laboratory. No One thinks about that. No One crunches the numbers. No One makes an impact. The fact that No One alters behavior in this ancient men's room has No One amazed.

The urinals are slightly more than five feet tall and extend down to the floor. No One feels the downward pitch of the tiles at the urinal's base. No One uses urinal eight for the hell of it. The urinal doesn't flush when No One turns and walks toward a sink. No One puts soiled hands underneath the automatic faucet. Nothing. No One waves hands in front of the paper towel dispenser. Nothing dispenses. No One walks to the door. No One ignores the "L" shaped device. No One grabs the door handle. No One opens the door.

Again, no one wonders about the butterfly effect.

KEVIN RABAS

About Barcellona

In a little town with one station master for the train called Barcellona, Sicily, where I ended up after a train strike and a cruel joke, a train switch, in Munich, I found the meaning of *perdido*, to be lost like in the Gillespie song. I'm sure the ticket woman thought I will teach this American something, send him to Barcellona, Sicily, instead of Barcelona, Spain, see how that fits him. In the wayside station, San Madre Familia, an old cathedral turned into a place for vagrants to rest the night, I slept in a room near a man who I thought was a wolf at first. His eyes– one red, one yellow– hit streetlight that night, and the length of the hair on his body hung thick. He did not rise from his bed but once during the night, and I tracked his motions with one eye open, a trick I had learned in the station in Rome, where I spent most of the day asleep with one eye open, because I had learned not to trust the dogs the police kept on chains. Drugs or no drugs, they would knock you over in your pack, if you let them. Stupid American, food in your pockets. Better yet fruit. They would inspect for that at the station, anything live or once living.

In Sicily, I stayed with the station master, and his family, after a night in San Madre Familia, the wayside station. When the station master called home, his daughter, who had dyed her hair red, hung up. He called again, a visitor here. Temporary. I'm bringing him home. And she, disowned for the day, was thankful. But first, drop him at the wayside station, find out what kind he is. In the morning, I opened San Madre Familia's green shutters and stood on the small veranda, and made one shot of the alley, the long Sicilian alley full of everyone's colorful laundry hanging, draped in a line that led to the head of the volcano, a god head. I shot with the Roleicord I had swapped a week of work for, developing, printing my mentor's work at the paper, and $25, payment, across town, in a church, I paid, and a woman left her Wiccan prayer circle for a moment, led me into a back room in the narthex, pulled the string on a purple Crown

Royal bag, and said, "It suits you, and you are so young. What is your name? Twenty-five dollars will be enough." This, this, when Dan, my mentor, said, "You have already paid." But she was beautiful, and it was late, around midnight, or 3, and I can't remember straight, and I had the cash on me, something else I learned about dealing with photographers: have the cash on you, if you want equipment, and you want it now, and you want it cheap, and you need it to shoot because you need the money, either for rent or for the love of a woman you know, caught in her apartment, who could use a boost, of tobacco, or cash, who could use what you have, right now, or she may just return to her drug, leave the bed, leave the room with the bolts on the door that is swung open only an inch, and I mean swung open in that city where I lived and loved a woman who almost taught me photography in the dark, the door shut and locked, she told me her dream: to teach me to agitate in the dark, her hands around my hands around the canisters full of water and developer and metal reels that held the negatives, swishing into being, but I declined, asked her instead to write for me, an editor at a small, small paper in the city, where the women, I could hear, said, "Damn, ain't he but a paperdoll from the back," and Amber was who I climbed steps for, who I walked sidewalks for, who I paced down alleys I should not have been in for, thinking of her in bed with a luke warm bottle of Cranapple juice beside her bed and a brown bag full of weed on the hardwood floor, there in her black skirt, black tights, and white polo shirt from the Rep. theatre, where she ushered nights so that she could practice her art at night, photography. Pink, nude, some called her work, pink porn artist, so minor. So wrong, of course, on term and love, on passion, on lust. What she wanted was the body, the body full out in love, and I knew this somewhat, although I was naïve enough to say once, "Yes, yes, I have come, and I am here for you, always, and, "No, she said. "Did you cum. It's wet down here" on her white Berber carpeted apartment, where she served fried chicken, gourmet, with spices, on white porcelain, or bone china, plates, with gold rims on the dishes as well as on the glasses in an apartment that had cracks in all the walls, and none of the windows shut out December, and we watched Taming the Shrew, the Taylor/Burton version on the couch, and then on the floor, tiring, and reviving, in that apartment. Amber, Amber, with her blue tule cloth hung over all the windows, draped so the red, red lights of the Sheridan came out purple into the room, the hotel that close to the windows that we prayed to it that night, to one night stands taking place, to love in the penthouse and on the lower floors, two strangers watching a video, and then Married with Children on the tube, when it came one, something I had never watched the entire way through before, and she laughed, and she laughed, and she laughed, and I didn't know then why, and I didn't laugh for her sake, but found something to rub on her back, a model's back, model's body. I had never touched one before, a body so full of her own life: she swam not for fitness but because it was the only way to keep the thing, the body, most alive. "It is not easy," she told me, "becoming, being, keeping this body. Careful, or you, too, will lose it. It's how I keep myself in this place," she'd say, in weaker moments, "while he is away in Europe. Yes, him, the composer, and yes, his is the same Kevin who looks so much like you I asked you two to stand together with him in the foyer so I could shoot you two and compare. And, yes, you are right. He should never know about you coming to see me, and yes, he did go crazy when I told him, and, yes, he was the one in the cage, dancing to techno in Pairs, the good one, while I kept the place up in KC, but would you have done otherwise, if you were me, you who I call O, and he who I call □. Music, it was his life, not the body, like you and me, and yours, yours, it is a boy's body with not so much hair. How is it you have lived this long in this city and have so little hair here?" And let her kiss my body, kiss my chest, and for each kiss, I promised her, a new hair would soon grow.

CLINT CHEREPA

The Chopping

I wanted to leave. I was wearied from staring at the same houses, their thatched roofs, gray and tired– fried by the unshielded sun. The occupants of the valley said I had roots and that I had no choice but to stay. What they said was half true, my well established tendrils gripped me to this location more and more each day. I needed to pull them up.

Before the sun had even burned away the morning mist my old friend, Blue, stopped by.

"Tomorrow I will go," I said.

"You've been saying that for the last ten years, and for some reason this time seems no different than the last," Blue said pouring himself three fingers of scotch. Blue never asked before he took. He believed what was mine was his. I had asked him about this once, but only once.

"If I don't drink it, who will?" he asked.

His argument was solid, as usual he left me with no retort. If he didn't use it, chances were I would, so on the risk of sounding selfish, I kept quiet.

"So what if I did go, what would you think of that?" I asked.

"Honestly, I think you wouldn't make it a mile before you toppled over dead," he said. "And why would you leave? You're the most powerful one living on this hill."

"As you can see there isn't much competition, besides, what's power without freedom?" I asked.

"Power," Blue replied. He then took a sip of scotch, rolled his head as he swirled it within his mouth, and asked, "Hey, have you been buying the cheap stuff?"

"If I'm that powerful, I think I should be able to buy whatever scotch I want, without comment," I said.

"Hmm, yep this is the cheap stuff."

I watched the silver sun fight from being pulled behind the stone cliffs across the valley. Blue happily downed his second tumbler.

He patted my shoulder and said, "I guess I best be on my way. Tomorrow?"

"Tomorrow, I'll see you tomorrow."

Long after the sun set, I stared into the sky pelleted with stars.

The only reason I had stayed here this long was patience. I had a glacier's patience. It was a quality of my fathers, his enduring patience, and it meant his death. Even though it brought his end, it was a quality I took pride in. Like him, I lived my whole life overlooking this valley.

I awoke to the scent of dew freshened clover. The cotton candy aroma made me crave tea sweetened with honey. I was covered in dew, as I had spent the night beneath stars, the way I had grown up doing. It depressed me to think how some had never spent a night unsheltered, free and unshackled from refuge.

Visitors were nonexistent on the hill. In truth, it had been years since anyone had visited besides Blue. I understood it was a long climb, and for what? I was the last one left living up here.

To disappear is my desire and my dream, but also my most dreaded fear.

Blue flew-in as the sun reached its apex and the shadows shrunk.

"Still here," he cockily cackled.

I held back the urge to smack him.

"Do you have any crackers?" he asked as he opened a pack of Limburger cheese.

"Afraid not," I said. I loved to tell him no.

Blue crunched crackers, and fed the ground more than his stomach.

"Last night I was telling the wife and kids about your grand aspiration," he said.

"And," I prompted.

"And they laid down their bets that you wouldn't get down to the bottom of the valley before you ran out of juice and turned back."

"They didn't say that," I retorted.

Blue looked as sheen as usual, his hair tight to his skull, and clothed in the only two colors he ever wore– blue and white.

He snapped at a cracker, "Yeah, your right, but that's how I feel."

My skin felt taunt from many days under the sun. I stretched my limbs. Blue took it as an act of aggression and instinctively hopped backwards.

"Do you think I would actually hit you?" I asked.

"No, you're not fast enough," Blue said. "So what's on the line up today? Are you up for a game of chess?"

"Sure."

The game was over within minutes. I don't know if Blue was just that bad, or I was that good. I never played against anyone else. Two moves before I had him in checkmate, he winged the board up into the air and declared the game a draw. It was classic Blue style. Our last thirty or more games were drawn in a similar manner.

Blue flew off in a huff, and neglected to thank me for the crackers and scotch.

The sun set and a chill fell upon the valley. The stone cottages lost smoke from their chimneys. I hated the smell of the smoke. Maple. This time of the year it was inevitable, the people grew cold and the smoke increased until I was stifled by the pollution twenty-four hours a day. It was a constant reminder of my need to leave.

The fumes of fear passed on from generation to generation. My first morbid memories of them shivered my extremities. I could leave these memories if only I could de-root, and unbind myself from this land.

I turned the idea over and then over again, the dream gaining speed, and it finally rolled into the valley itself, and splattered through the wood burning houses.

Blue could not understand. He had never been rooted. He flew and flew, and faced no hint of danger. The seriousness of my situation was lost in the mind of my only friend, Blue.

The dew landed in the form of frost during the night. I was calloused and accustomed to the cold. Forty years of sleeping in the open had a way of doing that. I absorbed the darkness and waited for the first crisp shrieks of the jays. The noxious fumes had slowed through the night, but soon pillaged the sky, they stood bright against the black canvas.

The village began to move with the task handlers. I watched one in particular. He came my way, leading a horse and a cart. A double sided axe bounced on his shoulder. He grew in size as he approached. No longer a speck, he stood stoutly at the base of my trunk. He circled. His beard glistened with perspiration. He wiped his hand across his beard and then raised the axe angled over his left shoulder.

Blue flew in with a shrill, "Nooooooooo."

But the man did not seem to understand.

CONTRIBUTORS

Joel Allegretti is the author of two full-length collections from *The Poet's Press*: *The Plague Psalms*, which appeared in 2000 and *Father Silicon* in 2006.

Christopher Beard received an undergraduate degree in poetry at the University of Kansas. He is currently a Doctoral Fellow at the University of North Texas and is working on his first book.

Jeremy D. Campbell studied literature at Michigan State University and has published fiction and poetry in *Word Riot* and *MAYDAY Magazine.* He currently lives in Seattle, Washington.

Terri Brown-Davidson's work has recently appeared in *The Virginia Quarterly Review.* She served as guest editor for *The Pedestal Magazine* and was a recipient of the New Mexico Writer's Scholarship for fiction.

Erika Brumett runs a portraiture business and is pursuing an MFA from Northwest Institute of Literary Arts: Whidbey Writers Workshop. Her words appear in *The Los Angeles Review* and *Soundings Review.*

Clint Cherepa is currently living in Nicaragua, writing, running and reading. He has written for TrailRunnner, Silent Sports, Wisconsin Trails and Marathon & Beyond.

Joe Clifford's work has appeared in *Fringe, Opium* and *Word Riot.* He is currently the producer of Lip Service West, a reading series in Oakland, CA.

Howie Good, a journalism professor at SUNY New Paltz, is the author of the full-length poetry collections Lovesick (*Press Americana*, 2009), Heart With a Dirty Windshield (*BeWrite Books*, 2010), and Everything Reminds Me of Me (*Desperanto*, 2011)

Bruce Harris is the author of *Sherlock Holmes and Doctor Watson: About Type.*

His fiction has appeared in *The First Line, elimae, Inch,* and *Pine Tree Mysteries.*

Ted Jean is a recently retired AIG executive. His work in *Pear Noir* was nominated for a Pushcart Prize.

Denis Joe has lived in Liverpool, England for the past 10 years and runs a poetry group for North End Writers.

Eddie Jones has been included in *The Harsh and The Heart* anthology from Bloomer Books and is upcoming in Space Squid Magazine. He lives in Grafton, Wisconsin with a woman who always has something for him to do.

Clare L. Martin is a poet/mother/wife, a graduate of the University of Louisiana at Lafayette and a lifelong Louisiana resident. Her poems appear in the 2011 Press 53 Spotlight anthology.

George Masters served with the Marine Corps in Vietnam and graduated from Georgetown University. His writing has appeared in the Boston Globe, Harvard's Charles River Review, Chicago Tribune and San Francisco Chronicle.

Stephen Mead is a published artist, writer and maker of short collage-films. His latest project is a two volume CD set of narrative poems entitled "Whispers of Arias".

Michael Milburn's writing has appeared most recently in *New England Review* and *Ploughshares.* He teaches English in New Haven, CT.

Mangesh Naik lives and works in Pune, India where he is currently working on a collection of ghost stories.

Kevin Rabas lives in Emporia, Kansas. He has one collection of short stories, *Spider Face.*

Mark Simpson's book, *A Poised World*, won the Rhea & Seymour Gorsline Poetry Competition from Bedbug Press in 2008. He works in Seattle as writer for an instructional design firm.

Mary Stone is an MFA student at the University of Kansas in Lawrence, where she teaches English classes and serves as a reader for *Beecher's* and the *Blue Island Review*.

Eloise Schultz is a student in New York City and winner of Instructor Magazine's 2007 poetry contest.

John Swain lives in Louisville, Kentucky. Thunderclap Press recently published his latest chapbook, *Fragments of Calendars*.

Made in the USA
Middletown, DE
25 January 2020